W9-CGY-483

BAROSAURUS

CAMARASAURUS

CERATOSAURUS

BRACHIOSAURUS

The stories from the
Dawn of time
Are told by ancient trees,

But stories that the
Bones can tell
Are older, far, than these.

# SHADOW *of the* DINOSAURS

## DENNIS NOLAN

SIMON & SCHUSTER BOOKS FOR YOUNG READERS

New York   London   Toronto   Sydney   Singapore

## *To the Bone Hunters*

Thank you to Noah and Kaper for sharing the adventure. And many thanks to paleontologists Daniel Chure, for his answers to my persistent questions, Daniel Brinkman, for checking dinosaurian facts, and especially Cynthia Marshall, for reading the manuscript, measuring sauropod and theropod skulls, and guiding me through the labyrinth of ancient dinosaur bones stored in the vaults of the Peabody Museum.

SIMON & SCHUSTER BOOKS FOR YOUNG READERS
An imprint of Simon & Schuster Children's Publishing Division
1230 Avenue of the Americas, New York, New York  10020
Copyright © 2001 by Dennis Nolan
All rights reserved including the right of reproduction in whole or in part in any form.
SIMON & SCHUSTER BOOKS FOR YOUNG READERS is a trademark of Simon & Schuster.
The text for this book is set in 18-point Life.
The illustrations are rendered in watercolor.
Printed in Hong Kong
10 9 8 7 6 5 4 3 2 1
Library of Congress Cataloging-in-Publication Data
Nolan, Dennis.
Shadow of the dinosaurs / by Dennis Nolan.—1st ed.
p.  cm.
Summary: A boy and his dog find a magic dinosaur bone
that shows them what life was like among the dinosaurs.
ISBN 0-689-82974-4
[1. Dinosaurs Fiction.  2. Magic Fiction.]  I. Title.
PZ7.N678Mag  2000  [E] 21   99-39786   CIP

**APATOSAURUS**

uh-PAT-uh-<u>SAW</u>-rus  70 ft. long

**BAROSAURUS**

BAYR-uh-<u>SAW</u>-rus  80 ft. long

**BRACHIOSAURUS**

BRACK-ee-uh-<u>SAW</u>-rus  82 ft. long

**CAMARASAURUS**

KAM-uh-ruh-<u>SAW</u>-rus  60 ft. long

**DIPLODOCUS**

di-PLOH-duh-kus  88 ft. long

**STEGOSAURUS**

STEG-uh-<u>SAW</u>-rus  25 ft. long

**ALLOSAURUS**

AL-uh-<u>SAW</u>-rus  40 ft. long

**CERATOSAURUS**

si-RAT-uh-<u>SAW</u>-rus  20 ft. long

**DERMODACTYLUS**  3 ft. wingspan

**DACHSHUND**  2 1/2 ft. long

The sun was beginning to set behind the mountains when Shadow saw the bone half buried in the rocky soil. Soon she pried it loose and ran back to where Jesse and his family were setting up camp for the night.

"Hey, Shadow," said Jesse. "What did you find?"

Jesse picked up the fossilized bone and turned it over in his hands. It was heavy and smooth to the touch.

"Shadow," he said, "I think this might be a dinosaur bone!"

After dinner, Jesse and Shadow sat before the crackling fire. Sparks flew into the black night as Jesse examined the ancient bone.

"I wonder what kind of dinosaur this might have come from," he said to Shadow. "Maybe a *Stegosaurus* . . . or a *Brachiosaurus* . . . or an *Allosaurus*!"

Shadow blinked her eyes.

"Don't you wish you could see them, Shadow?" Jesse sighed.

Shadow wagged her tail.

Jesse set the bone against the roots of an old gnarled tree and climbed into his sleeping bag.

"Sweet dreams, Shadow," he said.

Shadow curled up at Jesse's feet, and soon she and Jesse were fast asleep. Insects chirped and an owl hooted softly in the distance.

Then an odd humming sound woke Shadow. She looked at the dinosaur bone. It was glowing with a strange blue light, glowing and humming, louder and louder. The light brightened and spread up the old crooked trunk of the tree.

The entire grove soon shimmered with the eerie blue glow. The trees began to creak and moan from deep inside. Roots pulled free from the ground as the trees grew. Great knobby trunks became monstrous legs that stomped and shook the earth. Long tails sprouted and flicked about like wild snakes. At last, enormous necks shot into the air. Shadow darted in and out of the massive legs, barking and growling, but no one awoke.

Shadow stopped barking and stared up at the incredible long-necked dinosaurs towering over her. One curious *Diplodocus* lowered its head and sniffed at Shadow. A *Camarasaurus* did the same, then turned to walk away. A gigantic *Apatosaurus* followed, and soon the giant sauropods were moving slowly down the mountainside. One lone *Stegosaurus* lagged behind, swinging its spiked tail. Shadow carefully dodged its feet.

Then she heard the humming again.

The bone was glowing brightly next to a pile of broken boulders. Slowly the rocks, too, began to glow. They howled and roared as cracks ran through them. Fiery red eyes opened wide, serrated teeth filled powerful jaws, and claws like daggers scratched in the dirt. Shadow barked and barked as the boulders grew into ferocious theropods.

A spike-nosed *Ceratosaurus* snarled and pulled first one leg, then the other, from the stones. Another shook itself and roared loudly as a huge terrifying *Allosaurus* grew from the rocks. The *Allosaurus* stretched its legs, and spread its awful claws. Shadow growled. The *Allosaurus* lunged forward. Shadow turned and ran down the mountain. The dinosaurs screeched wickedly as they chased after her, straight toward the *Stegosaurus* and the sauropods.

Shadow dashed in between the sauropods' legs to hide. The *Allosaurus* was the first to reach them, mouth wide open and bellowing. Its many teeth flashed in the moonlight and its eyes shone like red hot coals. A *Ceratosaurus* stopped behind the *Allosaurus,* its tail switching back and forth. Another grumbled and pawed angrily at the dirt with its claws. Then they charged forward.

The theropods came to a stop as a tremendous *Brachiosaurus* turned to face them. A giant *Barosaurus* pounded its feet heavily on the ground, and the other sauropods snapped their tails like whips. Step-by-step the mighty dinosaurs moved closer and closer to each other. Thick black storm clouds rolled across the sky, and thunder rumbled in the distance. Shadow shivered in terror as the *Allosaurus* screamed. One after another, the dinosaurs began to howl until the mountainside resounded with their fearsome cries.

Shadow crept from underneath the sauropods and ran back up the trail to find the dinosaur bone. Pterosaurs cackled and flapped at her with their leathery wings as she searched the mountainside. A volcano, rising from the ground, filled the sky with heavy clouds of ash. At last Shadow found the bone, glowing dimly among the dark rocks, and began to dig.

Suddenly, the volcano exploded with a deafening blast. Rivers of red boiling lava poured from cracks in its side. The ground trembled and the dinosaurs ran wildly through the hot air as Shadow dug deeper. Finally she dropped the dinosaur bone into the hole.

Shadow kicked dirt into the hole until the bone was buried. The volcano wheezed and sputtered and flattened back into the earth. With one last puff of smoke, it was gone. The dinosaurs moaned and whined as they changed back into the rocks and trees they had been. Storm clouds blew away and a quiet stillness returned to the mountain. The sun was just beginning to rise as an exhausted Shadow ran to find Jesse, still sleeping peacefully at the campsite.

Jesse rolled over and opened his eyes.

"Shadow," he said, "I just had the wildest dream! There were all kinds of dinosaurs! An *Apatosaurus,* and a *Diplodocus,* and an *Allosaurus,* and a volcano, and YOU were there, and the bone . . ."

Jesse looked to where he had set the bone the night before.

"Shadow, have you seen the bone?" asked Jesse. "Shadow? Shadow?"

But Shadow was curled up at Jesse's feet, sound asleep.

# AUTHOR'S NOTE

The enormous dinosaurs in this book were all quite real once. The mighty meat-eating theropods: *Allosaurus* and *Ceratosaurus;* the gigantic plant-eating sauropods: *Apatosaurus, Barosaurus, Brachiosaurus, Camarasaurus,* and *Diplodocus;* and the strange spike-tailed *Stegosaurus* could all have been found living 145 million years ago, in what is present-day North America. The *Dermodactylus,* a pterosaur, was a type of flying reptile closely related to the dinosaurs.

The bones of dinosaurs have been found on every continent, including Antarctica. Many different kinds of dinosaurs appeared and disappeared throughout the entire length of the Mesozoic Era, which lasted more than 160 million years. At the dawn of the Cenozoic Era, 65 million years ago, most of the great dinosaurs were gone. The reason for their final disappearance remains a mystery.

APATOSAURUS

STEGOSAURUS

ALLOSAURUS

DIPLODOCUS